Contents

Welcome to Mermaids Rock!

The Emerald Maze

Linda Chapman

Illustrated by Mirelle Ortega

LITTLE TIGER

LONDON

Naya &
Octavia
Coralie & Dash
Luna &
Melly

Chapter One
Trouble on the Reef

"Found another one!" Flicking her silvery green tail, Marina Silverfin dived triumphantly down through the clear turquoise water. She pointed at a pale gold starfish with five slender arms that was perfectly camouflaged against the base of a yellow sea fan. "Mark another brittle-star down on our chart, Naya."

Sami, her pet seahorse, bobbed in and out of the sea fan's branches, disturbing a timid, stripy butterfly fish that swam up past Marina's nose.

Naya used her squid-ink pen to put another tally mark in the column headed 'Brittle Starfish' in her notebook. The Save the Sea Creatures Club – Marina, Naya, Coralie, Kai and Luna – had come out on the coral reef that morning to conduct a study for Luna's mum, Erin. Erin worked at the Marine Sanctuary on the remote reef where the merpeople lived. She had told them that the number and variety of starfish were good indicators of how healthy the reef was and so now they were investigating the starfish population in three different areas.

The gang all loved helping to protect their beautiful home and the fish and marine mammals that lived there. They picked up plastic litter that had washed up on to the reef so that it didn't cause any damage; they rescued any animals that were in trouble and they had even made nesting boxes for the tiny sea dragons and seahorses so their young could hatch in peace.

Octavia, Naya's pet octopus, pulled at her arm and pointed to where a bright red starfish with black tips at the ends of its arms was clinging on tightly to a boulder covered in orange lichen.

"A young Indian sea star. Thanks, Octavia," called Naya, marking it down. "Well spotted!" Octavia waved her arms in a happy dance.

Luna was floating a little way off, gently separating a clump of tube-like green and blue sponges, her eyes scanning for starfish, while her pet manatee, Melly, grazed on a nearby patch of seagrass. Coralie and Kai were whispering together while Dash, Coralie's young bottlenose dolphin, and Tommy, Kai's hawksbill turtle, played hide-and-seek round the coral.

"Are you two going to help?" Naya called to Coralie and Kai.

Coralie sighed and pushed back her long dark red hair. "I do like looking after the reef, but this is a bit too much like schoolwork. Surely we've done enough now?"

"Coralie and I might race to the Cuttlefish Cave," said Kai. "We'll do some litter picking when we get there."

"OK," said Marina. "You go. We'll finish off here." She, Naya and Luna loved doing research – particularly if it helped keep the coral reef healthy – but Coralie and Kai much preferred to be more active. "We'll meet you there when we're done."

"Naya, can we borrow a lantern in case the cave is really dark?" Coralie asked.

"Of course! Help yourself," said Naya, nodding to her seaweed bag that was on a nearby rock.

Naya was fascinated by science and was always inventing things. A little while ago, she had come up with the idea of making lanterns using a liquid made from ground sea pansy and bioluminescent algae. She had discovered that when the algae liquid was mixed with magic mermaid powder it caused a bright light to shine and she had used this to create emergency lanterns. She'd invented lots of other useful things too, including a powerful iron tonic that allowed sea mammals like dolphins and manatees to stay underwater for longer.

Her most recent invention was glow-in-the-dark paint. It had been inspired by an adventure the gang had had in the Midnight

Zone – the deepest, darkest, most dangerous part of the ocean where many of the fish and other creatures had glowing bodies. The gang had had a very scary time down there and had only just managed to avoid being eaten by a giant squid!

Coralie and Kai rummaged inside Naya's seaweed bag, then called goodbye and sped away.

Marina glanced over to where Luna was now stroking a baby manta ray who had swum up from the ocean floor to say hello to her. All sea creatures loved Luna. She only had to hum and they would come flocking to her to be petted.

Marina smiled. Luna was a few years younger than the rest of the Save the Sea Creatures gang, but her talent was amazingly useful to them on their adventures.

"I think we've finished on this section of the reef," said Naya, swimming over and picking her bag up. “Let’s move on.”

A shoal of small red, white and purple firefish came flickering past and Marina let them sweep her on to the next part of the reef. For a moment, all she could see was a cloud of tiny bright fish around her and then the shoal rushed on its way and she was left alone.

She, Naya and Luna spent the following twenty minutes scouring the next section of the reef, noting down all the starfish they saw, and then they headed over to meet Coralie and Kai at the cave where the cuttlefish had their babies once a year. The opening of the cave gaped like a dark mouth, but there was no sign of their friends nearby.

“Where are they?” asked Naya.

Octavia held up her arms in a helpless gesture.

“Maybe they’re inside the cave,” said Marina.

They swam in through the entrance and, as they were swallowed up by the darkness, Marina's blood turned to ice. A giant, glowing green squid was squatting at the back of the cave! Its arms were raised above its head and it had ferocious teeth that seemed to shine.

"Quick, get out!" she cried, as Luna shrieked.

"Swim! Go on!" Marina shouted, pushing her friends out in front of her, desperate to get them to safety.

But, as she urged them away, she heard the sound of smothered giggling. Marina spun round. Kai and Coralie popped out from behind a rock on one side of the cave. Their hands were covering their mouths and their shoulders were shaking as they tried to contain their laughter.

"What's going on?" Marina demanded suspiciously.

"We tricked you!" Coralie exclaimed.

"It's not a real squid! We drew it with Naya's glow-in-the-dark paint!" spluttered Kai, holding up a pot of paint and a brush. "We took it out of her bag when we borrowed a lantern."

"You should have seen your face, Marina!" said Coralie. "You looked as shocked as a blobfish that's just caught sight of itself in a mirror!"

Marina saw the funny side and joined in with their laughter.

Naya and Luna swam back into the cave. "What's happening?" demanded Naya.

"I *ink* –" Coralie winked at Kai – "Kai and I just tricked you!"

She and Kai explained their trick and soon

they were all giggling.

"Well, that wasn't exactly the purpose I had in mind when I invented it," said Naya, shaking her head and taking the paint from Kai. "It's supposed to be for marking our way if we're exploring somewhere dark."

"Playing pranks with it is way more fun!" said Coralie, her eyes sparkling. "We should use it to trick Glenda."

Glenda Seagrass was a blonde mergirl in their class at school. She and her friends used to be mean to Marina and the others, but a little while ago the Savc the Sea Creatures gang had stopped Glenda from getting into trouble and since then she had been much friendlier.

Naya shook her head. "Glenda's being nice at the moment – we shouldn't be horrible to her."

"Oh, but she's so easy to wind up. It's fun!" said Coralie.

"Well, we're not wasting the paint that's left to play a trick on her,' said Naya firmly, putting it back in her bag. "I only managed to make this pot because your dad –" she looked at Marina – "let me have some silver powder and a rock called sphalerite after I told him my idea for creating glow-in-the-dark paint."

Tarak, Marina's father, was a marine research scientist and on his travels he had collected things from all over the world. He encouraged Naya with her inventions and often lent her books and ingredients.

"I guess I should go and find Mum," said Luna, stroking Melly, who waggled her flippers happily. "She'll start to worry if I'm out much longer."

"We'll come with you," said Naya. "We can tell her what we discovered about the starfish numbers."

"And we can see if she wants any help with the animals," said Marina. She loved helping out at the Marine Sanctuary with the ill, injured and orphaned animals. At the moment, there was an incredibly cute baby dolphin called Bubbles who Marina and Sami loved to play with.

"I'll have to go home," sighed Coralie. "I haven't done our weekend homework yet."

"Me neither," said Kai. "I like school but I hate homework."

"I love it," said Naya.

"You can do mine for me if you like," said Coralie hopefully.

"Nope," said Naya, shaking her head. "You know you have to do it yourself. And this weekend it's really interesting. It's all about the properties of different rocks and minerals. It's fascinating."

Coralie grinned. "You're as crazy as a crayfish, Naya! It's lucky we're all so different because that's what makes us such a *fin-tastic* team!" She turned to Kai. "Come on, let's do our homework together. Race you back to the caves!"

Kai grabbed Tommy's shell and the turtle zoomed off. Coralie and Dash charged after them.

Marina, Naya and Luna set off more slowly in the direction of the Marine Sanctuary, weaving through the sea fans and swimming over beds of flower-like pink and purple anemones where friendly orange-and-white clownfish searched for food. The warm waters of the coral reef teemed with life. Leatherback and hawksbill turtles glided past them, crabs

and lobsters picked their way across the seabed, shoals of small fish swooped by and larger, slower fish weaved in and out of the coral.

Naya, Luna, Coralie and Kai had lived there all their lives, but Marina had only moved to the reef a year ago. Before that, she and her dad had travelled round the world together while he did his research. Marina had loved visiting other places, but she was really enjoying staying in one place, going to school and having friends for the first time in her life.

In the distance, she could see Mermaids Rock – a massive rock shaped like a mermaid's tail that jutted up from the seabed. It marked the entrance to the merpeople's shallow-water reef and had a magic whirlpool swirling round at its base. The whirlpool linked to a network of smaller whirlpools all over the world and the merpeople could use it to get to wherever they wanted. All they had to do was touch the rock, say where they wanted to go and dive in. Today, there was a large group of guards swimming beside it as well as the Chief of the Guards, Razeem. He had a pointed beard and his blue eyes were very sharp.

"I wonder what's going on over there?" said Naya curiously. The guards looked worried and Razeem was frowning as he peered intently at the swirling waters of the whirlpool. It seemed to be spinning faster than usual, the water bubbling and frothing madly.

"Let's go and find out!" said Marina and they swam over.

Indra, Kai's mum, who was one of the guards, had her arm round a bedraggled mermaid. She was sobbing and Indra was comforting her. "It's OK, Freya. You're back now, you're safe."

"But it was so horrible!" cried Freya. "It was really dark and I couldn't see a thing. I tried to come back, but the whirlpool disappeared. I thought I was going to be trapped in the dark forever!"

"What's going on?" Marina asked inquisitively.

Chief Razeem swung round. "No children allowed! It's far too dangerous. You need to leave!"

"But what's happening?" Marina persisted.

"In the name of Neptune, I said leave!" Chief Razeem roared.

Naya and Luna tugged her arms. "Come on, Marina," Naya urged.

Marina scowled. She hated being ordered about and she desperately wanted to find out what was going on.

"Marina, please do what the chief says," Indra said, swimming over. "It really is too dangerous here at the moment and Chief Razeem will get very angry if you don't go."

Marina gave in and reluctantly let the others pull her away.

Chapter Two
Bubbles the Baby Dolphin

As Marina, Naya and Luna turned to swim away, they almost bumped into a mergirl who was combing her long blonde hair while examining her reflection in a mirror made out of mother-of-pearl.

"Be careful!" she exclaimed.

"Whoops, sorry, Glenda!" said Naya.

"You almost made me drop my mirror and comb. Look at them – I got them for my birthday yesterday," said Glenda. "Aren't they beautiful?" She held them out proudly.

"I guess so," said Marina. She didn't see the appeal of combs and mirrors. "Happy birthday for yesterday, Glenda! Do you know what's going on at the whirlpool?" she went on as Glenda fixed the comb in her hair and slipped the mirror into her pink seaweed bag. "Has your dad said anything?" Chief Razeem was Glenda's father.

"You mean you three don't know?" said Glenda, slightly smugly.

"No," said Marina.

"There was a mermaid by the whirlpool who looked really upset," said Naya.

"What had happened to her?" asked Luna. "Why was she crying?"

"Well –" Glenda leaned forwards, looking keen to share what

she knew – "I'm not surprised that she was upset. She had asked the whirlpool to take her to the South Pacific Ocean but, when she dived in, it spun super-fast and she ended up somewhere pitch-black. Definitely not the South Pacific Ocean. She didn't know where she was and then the whirlpool she should have been able to use to come back just disappeared. It vanished!"

"Flippers! What did she do?" breathed Marina. This was fascinating: she'd never heard of the whirlpool malfunctioning before.

Glenda flicked her hair. "After twenty minutes, the whirlpool reappeared. She dived into it and it brought her home. Daddy is trying to find out what happened. In the meantime, no one is allowed to use the whirlpool."

"But that's awful," said Naya.

Luna nodded. "If the grown-ups can't use it, that means they can't help out in all the different oceans."

"I know and it also means we won't be able to go on any more school trips until the problem is sorted," Glenda said with a sigh. "I loved it when we all went camping on the coral atoll. It's the only time Daddy's ever allowed me off the reef." She looked at Marina enviously. "You're so lucky to have travelled all over the place and to have had so many adventures."

Marina nodded. She knew she was really lucky to have seen so much of the world. "Does anyone know why the whirlpool isn't working properly?" she asked.

"No, Daddy and the rest of the guards are trying to work it out at the moment," said Glenda. "They're going to call a meeting for all the adults, to tell them no one must use the whirlpool."

As she spoke, there was the sound of a conch shell being blown – three long blasts followed by three shorts ones, a pattern that was repeated several times. It was a signal that the adult merpeople should gather in the large open area near the school.

"I'd better get to the sanctuary and tell Mum I'm OK before she goes off to the meeting," said Luna.

"We'll come with you," said Naya. "See you, Glenda!"

They hurried away, zipping between the gliding turtles and avoiding a flame scallop that was propelling itself through the water by clapping the two sides of its sharp shell together. The Marine Sanctuary was very close to the meeting area and, when they got there, Luna's mum was still seeing to the animals. She had Bubbles, the young dolphin, on a long lead made of seaweed and was practising getting him to come when called. It seemed to be going well. Bubbles was racing back eagerly every time Erin called his name and getting praise and pats.

"Ah, there you are!" she said, spotting Luna and the others. "I'm glad you're back. I don't know what's going on, but it sounds like there's a meeting I have to go to."

"It's about the whirlpool," Marina said. "It's not working properly."

"Chief Razeem has banned people from using it," said Luna. She hugged Melly. "I'm glad we weren't in it when it went wrong. It would be so scary to get trapped somewhere dark and not be able to get back."

Melly nuzzled her comfortingly.

"Oh dear," said Erin, looking worried. "I was just about to take Bubbles for a swim, but I must go to the meeting. I don't know how long it will go on for so you'd better head home to our cave and wait for me there, Luna."

"Naya and I could take Bubbles out for you," Marina offered. "We don't have to go home yet."

"Yes, we'd like to help," Naya said, stroking the baby dolphin, who blew a stream of bubbles excitedly out of his blowhole.

Erin beamed at them. "*Fin-tastic!* Thank you, girls!" She handed the lead over. "Be careful – he's stronger than he looks. He's definitely ready to leave the sanctuary and go to a new home now so, if you hear of anyone looking for a pet dolphin, let me know."

Bubbles bounced round Marina, tugging at the lead. He'd been quite timid when he first came to the sanctuary, but now his confidence had grown and he was very playful.

"Oh no you don't,' said Marina, hanging on with two hands. "You're not getting away from me. See you later, Erin. Bye, Luna."

"I wish I could come with you," said Luna.

"You can take Bubbles out another time," Erin reassured her.

Marine and Naya waved goodbye, then took Bubbles away from where the adults were gathering. Octavia kept teasing Bubbles by darting at him and then swimming away just out of reach and waving cheekily. Bubbles tried to leap at her, almost yanking the lead out of Marina's hands. "He really is strong," she said. "Octavia, you're not helping."

Octavia blew a cloud of ink at Marina and shot over to Naya. She wrapped her arms round Naya's neck. "You're so naughty," Naya told her.

Octavia shook as if she was laughing.

"I've had an idea," Marina said slowly, wondering what Naya would think. "Why don't we go over to the whirlpool?"

Naya stared at her. "But we're not allowed near it. You heard what the chief and Indra said."

"I know. We won't go close, but don't you want to see it? I wonder what can be making it go wrong," Marina said.

"There's got to be some sort of magical disturbance causing it to malfunction," said Naya thoughtfully. "Magic is a form of energy. It can be channelled or contained, but the flow can also be disrupted. I wonder what's happening in the whirlpool."

"It's a real mystery, isn't it?" said Marina, watching her closely. She knew Naya didn't like breaking the rules, but she also knew how much she loved solving mysteries.

"It is," said Naya. She hesitated and then grinned. "OK, we can go closer to it, but not too close. Agreed?"

Marina flicked her tail in delight. She'd been hoping Naya wouldn't be able to resist investigating further. "Agreed! Come on, Bubbles!"

Glenda was perched on a large, smooth boulder near Mermaids Rock. "Where are you two going?" she called as they swam past. "And why have you got that dolphin? You haven't got another pet, have you?"

"No, Bubbles is an orphan. We're exercising him for Erin," Marina explained.

Bubbles lunged towards Glenda, keen to say hello.

"Keep it away!" gasped Glenda, shrinking back.

Marina remembered that Glenda didn't like dolphins or porpoises ever since she'd borrowed one for a pet talent contest and it had dragged her into a cake stall. "Don't worry, Glenda. Bubbles is just a baby. He wants to be friends –

look how sweet he is."

"Why don't you say hello?" said Naya.

"I suppose he is quite cute," said Glenda. Reluctantly, she reached out with one hand and patted Bubbles on the head. "Hello there, baby dolphin." Bubbles clicked his tongue at her and pushed his head against Glenda's tail.

"What's he doing that for?" Glenda asked warily.

"It's his way of greeting you," said Naya.

"Good boy, Bubbles," praised Marina. "You're being very well behaved."

"Can I hold his lead?" Glenda asked.

"OK, but hang on tight," said Marina,

handing it over.

Glenda took the lead and stroked the dolphin's face. Bubbles whistled happily. "You like that, don't you?" cooed Glenda. She smiled and tickled Bubbles under the chin. "Oh yes, you do, you really do!"

Getting overexcited by all the fussing, Bubbles leaped up eagerly, pushing his nose into Glenda's face. Glenda hadn't been expecting the sudden movement and she screamed loudly in surprise. She had the loudest scream of any of the merchildren on the reef and Bubbles shot backwards in shock, pulling the lead out of Glenda's fingers. Realizing he was free, he raced off towards Sami and Octavia who were swimming near the whirlpool.

"No, Bubbles!" shouted Naya. "Stop!"

Marina remembered the training that Erin had been doing when they saw her at the sanctuary. "Bubbles, come!" she yelled.

"Come on, Bubbles! Come back!"

For one awful moment, she thought Bubbles was going to jump straight into the whirlpool but, hearing the familiar command, he stopped and swung round. Marina felt a tidal wave of relief. Then, to her horror, she saw Bubble's tail fin hit little Sami. The seahorse flew through the water, straight into the swirling whirlpool.

Marina let out a shriek almost as loud as Glenda's. She raced over, but Sami had gone!

Chapter Three

In the Dark

"Sami!" Marina yelled. Without a moment's hesitation, she dived into the whirlpool after the golden seahorse. She'd travelled using the whirlpool plenty of times, but this felt completely different. The water spun her round and round faster than it ever had done before, grabbing and clawing at her angrily. She felt like it wanted to tear her limb from limb. She forced her eyes open but all she could see was an inky blackness. She never usually felt scared but now fear rushed through her.

With a gasp, she shot out into pitch-dark cold water. She blinked but couldn't see a thing. Fear gripped her. Where was she? More importantly, where was Sami? Had the whirlpool brought them both to the same place?

"Sami!" she called anxiously, keeping her voice low. Her stomach twisted with nerves. The only place she had ever been before that was as dark as this was the Midnight Zone and all sorts of dangerous creatures lived there. "Sami!" she hissed, desperately wishing she had a light so she could see where she was. Was she in the Midnight Zone again?

But no. She suddenly realized she wasn't in salt water. This was fresh water, which meant she wasn't in the sea. Maybe she was in a river somewhere. Why would a river be so dark though? It could be night-time, but then surely she'd catch the light of stars twinkling high overhead through the surface of the water. She was about to swim up to have a look when she felt something brush against her cheek.

For one awful moment, she thought that it was a giant squid's tentacle, but then a dark, seahorse-shaped shadow bobbed in front of her face and she felt Sami's little snout press against the end of her nose. It was his way of kissing her. "Sami!" she gasped with a sharp sting of relief. She cupped her hands round the little seahorse in delight. "Oh, Sami, I was so scared! I thought I'd lost you, that maybe we'd ended up in different places. I'm so glad you're here – and that you're OK!"

She kissed the top of his forehead and he rubbed his cheek against her fingers and waggled his horns. Before Marina had gone to live on the reef at Mermaids Rock, Sami had been her only friend and she didn't know what she'd do without him.

"Where do you think we are?" she whispered.

Sami shook his little head.

"Well, I guess it doesn't matter," said Marina. "Now I've found you we can go home." She could hear the whirlpool swirling swiftly beneath them, the water bubbling and hissing. She tucked Sami behind her ear and felt his tail twirl tightly round a lock of her shoulder-length brown hair. "Hold tight!"

She was just about to dive down to the frothing whirlpool when suddenly a shape came flying out. Marina froze. Who or what was it?

"H-hello?" she stammered.

There was the sound of rummaging and then a light flared in the darkness. "Marina?" said a familiar voice.

Marina felt a rush of relief as she saw it was Naya. Octavia was hanging on to Naya's neck and Naya was holding up an emergency lantern. She had activated it and it was now sparkling with light, illuminating the gloom.

"Oh, Naya!" cried Marina, racing over. They hugged each other. "What are you doing here?"

"When I saw you jump in after Sami, I followed you," said Naya. "I left Bubbles with Glenda and dived straight into the whirlpool with Octavia. It went really fast, didn't it?" She touched her dark braids, checking the beads at the ends were all in place, then she held the lantern up. "Where do you think we are, Marina? What is this place?"

"I have no idea. I was just going to swim to the surface to try and work it out," said Marina. "It looks just like the place that

Freya was describing to the guards though. Come on, let's see if we can find out more!" With Naya and Octavia there, she felt suddenly much braver and more confident.

The two mergirls swam up to the surface with their pets. When they popped their heads out of the still, cold water, Naya swung her light around and they saw that they were in a cave made of pale rocks with a very high, craggy ceiling arching overhead. Long, knobbly stalactites hung down over the water, like giant fangs. There was a slit of light at the very top of the cave, a hole that seemed to lead to the outside world. An old and decaying rope ladder hung down from it, reaching all the way to a wide, rocky ledge that jutted out from the side of the cave, just beneath the surface of the water.

Diving back under, they examined the ledge. It was covered with green algae and its end was jagged as if part of it had broken away. On the ledge there were a couple of strange objects.

Marina swam nearer to investigate. "Look at these, Naya," she called. There was a small stone statue with a human-shaped body, and a stone pot lying on its side. Marina could see ornate carvings and patterns on the sides of the pot, but it was cracked and the water had worn away some of the detail. On the cave wall, behind the shelf, there were lots of painted handprints.

"This must be a place where humans come," said Marina uneasily. The merpeople were supposed to keep away from them at all costs.

"Or once came," said Naya thoughtfully. "It doesn't seem like anyone has been here for ages. Look at how old and broken the rope ladder is. Lots of the rungs are missing. There's no way a human would be able to get down it now. I think we're safe."

"But why did humans come into this cave and leave that stuff and make those handprints?" said Marina.

"I've absolutely no idea," said Naya. "But I think I know where we might be. I've read about underground rivers like this one. They flow beneath the ground, forming pools in caves. Sometimes the rooves of the caves collapse and the river appears in the open before vanishing underground again. Open caves like that are called cenotes."

"Which part of the world are we in then?" said Marina, intrigued. She'd been to lots of places, but she'd never heard of underground rivers and cenotes.

"I'm not absolutely sure, but I know there are quite a lot of underground rivers and cenotes in Mexico, in North America," said Naya. "So maybe we're there." She looked torn. "If we swam on a bit – following the river – we'd see more and we might find out for sure..."

"Let's do it!" Marina said instantly.

"Or perhaps we should go back," Naya said,

with a slightly nervous glance at the whirlpool beneath them. "What if that whirlpool disappears while we're exploring?"

"Freya said it disappeared for a while but then came back again," said Marina. "I think we should risk it. We might never have a chance to come somewhere like this again."

Naya grinned. "OK, let's swim down the river and see what we find!"

Chapter Four
Exploring!

Marina and Naya swam to where the river left the cave, using Naya's lantern to light the way. They followed it down a wide tunnel. Octavia swam beside them, her eight arms trailing behind her, while Sami hitched a lift in Marina's hair. She could feel his little horns wiggling inquisitively against her neck. None of them had ever swum in anything like this dark, tranquil, underground river before. The water was clear, just like the water on their coral reef, but it was much colder and there was hardly anything to be seen apart from pale rock formations. Marina thought of the colour and life on their reef at home – the banks of bright coral and sea sponges, the shoals of fish, the turtles, the friendly manatees and porpoises. This was a completely different underwater world from the one they were used to, a strange world that was quiet and still.

The tunnel opened out into another cave. This one had a lower roof and stalactites that were so long they jabbed down through the surface of the water like spears. Marina, Naya and Octavia weaved round them, avoiding their sharp, dangerous points. At the far end of the cave, the river split, heading down two separate tunnels. "Let's take the bigger one!" Marina said, speeding up.

"Wait, Marina!" Naya called anxiously. "I think we should mark our way with paint. If there are lots of tunnels, we could get lost and not be able to find our way back."

"We'll remember," said Marina. "Come on!"

She raced on confidently, leaving Naya behind. The tunnel twisted and turned. She took a left fork and found herself in a new cave. This one was long and narrow with a slim opening to the outside world in the craggy roof. There was a natural rocky ledge that ran along one side of the cave, just above the surface of the water, and on it were piles of old ivory-coloured bones that seemed to glow in the dim, gloomy light. A shiver, partly of excitement and partly of fear, tingled down Marina's spine. How had those bones got there? These caves were so strange and spooky!

With a flick of her tail, she swam on. The next cave was pitch-black. Marina stopped as she swam into it, her heart starting to beat a bit more quickly. What if there was something lurking in the dark, something that was just waiting to pounce?

She began to wish she hadn't swum on so quickly on her own. She poked her head out of the water and looked back. "Naya! Where are you?" she shouted.

To her astonishment, part of the cave roof suddenly seemed to detach itself. It split into hundreds of small dark shapes with wings. The cave was filled with high-pitched squeaks as the winged creatures flew at her, tangling in her hair. Marina shrieked and ducked underwater, covering her ears with her hands. What were these things?

She swam back the way she had come as fast as possible, but when she reached the fork in the tunnel she couldn't remember which way she'd come. Panic raced through her as she looked from one tunnel to the other. She was in the dark and she was lost! Images of fantastical monsters flooded her mind – monsters that ate people and turned them into piles of bones; monsters that could split themselves into hundreds of tiny, shrieking shapes and attack!

An octopus suddenly zoomed up in front of her nose.

"Octavia!" Marina gasped. Seeing Octavia's familiar shape, her panic faded slightly. "Where's Naya? Can you take me to her?" she said quickly.

Octavia nodded and beckoned to Marina. She led the way back to the cave where Marina had left Naya. Marina felt a rush of relief when she saw her friend. She swam over and hugged her. "Thanks so much for sending Octavia after me. I got lost."

"I heard you shout, but I didn't know where you were. I was really worried," said Naya. "Don't go off again – please!"

"I won't, I promise," said Marina. "This place is amazing but really weird."

She told Naya about the bones and the strange creatures in the cave.

"I don't know how the bones got there, but I bet the flying creatures were bats," said Naya. "Bats hang upside down from cave rooves. When you shouted, you would have woken them all up."

Marina gave a shudder as she remembered the way the bats had swooped at her head. "Let's take the other tunnel next time."

Naya grinned. "I think the bats might prefer that. You must have given them quite a shock!"

"Poor bats," said Marina, feeling sorry for them now she knew what they were.

"From now on, we mark the way we're going," Naya said firmly. She pulled out the pot of glow-in-the-dark paint and a brush and painted a green arrow on the wall of the tunnel they were going to take. It led to a cave with a roof so low that it almost touched the surface of the water, then to a cave with a hole at the top that let in shafts of sunlight. They journeyed on through the network of caves and tunnels, painting arrows as they went.

"Look, it's really bright ahead!" Naya said, pointing to the end of the tunnel they were in. Light was flooding in. They increased their speed and burst out into a circle of glittering, sunlit water. Looking round, Marina saw that they were in a large pool surrounded by rocks. Trees with slender trunks leaned low over the water, their green fronds very big and wide. Thick vines scrambled over tree trunks and brushed the surface of the water. Through the trees, dense jungle stretched away on all sides.

"Oh, barnacles!" breathed Marina. "What is this place?"

"I think this pool must once have been in a cave," Naya said. "But I guess, over time, the roof fell in and now it's open to the sky and jungle. Look, the river goes back underground again over there." She pointed across the pool. "Should we swim on?"

"No, I want to explore here," said Marina. With a few flicks of her tail, she reached the rocky edge of the pool. The air was warm and humid and she breathed in the unfamiliar smell of plants, soil and trees. "I've never seen a jungle before." She gazed around. She was so used to being in the sea, it felt very strange to be surrounded by land. A shiver of unease ran through her – land meant humans. *I hope there aren't any nearby*, she thought anxiously.

Overhead, blue, yellow and red birds were swooping through the trees, calling out with cackles and cries, their wings bright splashes of colour against the leafy canopy. A giant dragonfly zoomed past, its iridescent wings and deep blue body glittering in the sunlight. It was joined by another, and then two huge butterflies with creamy wings fluttered together above the surface of the pool and landed on a bush that was covered with large pink flowers.

Marina gently untangled Sami from her hair and placed him in the water – unlike

merpeople, seahorses could only breathe underwater – then she pulled herself out of the water on to the rocks. For the first time in her life, she wished she had legs so she could go exploring through the trees! Instead, she had to content herself with looking at everything.

"There are so many different plants," said Naya excitedly, pulling herself out beside a dense patch of bushes. "Ow!" She shook her hand suddenly.

"Are you OK?" Marina asked.

"Yes, I'm fine. I scraped my hand on a rock. It's just a graze." Naya reached into the bushes and started examining the different leaves. "I wonder if the leaves here are like seaweed and all have different properties," she said. "I heard humans make medicines out of leaves just like we do out of seaweed." She peered at them curiously. "I wish I knew what they all were."

Marina was more interested in the wildlife than the plants. She'd seen lots of birds before, but only seabirds. She'd never seen anything like these brightly coloured birds flying through the trees or the black bird with a huge multicoloured beak that was watching her curiously from a nearby bush.

Marina pulled herself along the rocks, edging closer to it. "What type of bird are you then?" she said softly. As she got close, the branches parted and a strange furry head poked out. For a moment, she almost thought it was a human. The creature had a wrinkled face with pale grey circles around bright dark eyes.

Marina shrieked in shock and threw herself back into the water. Heart pounding, she watched as the creature leaped on to a nearby tree trunk and then swung away from branch to branch, using its furry legs, arms and tail to balance. "What was that?" she gasped, pointing.

"A monkey," said Naya, giggling. "I've read about them in books!"

"This place is just awesome!" said Marina, recovering quickly from her shock and turning a somersault in delight. "Oh, I wish the others were with us. They'd love it!"

"I almost don't want to go back," said Naya, slipping into the water and swimming over to her. "There's so much to see."

Marina reached out to take her hands and swing her round in delight, but then remembered Naya's scrape and stopped herself. "Sorry, I forgot about your hand. How is it now?"

Naya checked. "It's stopped bleeding and it's nearly disappeared." She frowned. "That's strange that it should heal so quickly..."

She broke off as they both heard a faint but very familiar high-pitched scream, coming from the direction they had swum in. They looked at each other.

"Glenda!" they both exclaimed at the same time.

"I'd know that scream anywhere," said Marina. "She must have come through the whirlpool too!"

"We'd better go back," said Naya. "She'll be in the dark all on her own."

Then they heard two other people shouting.

"She isn't alone, Naya!" exclaimed Marina. "That sounds like Coralie and Kai. Come on!"

Chapter Five

Racing to the Rescue

Marina and Naya zoomed back through the network of caves and tunnels. Thanks to Naya's glow-in-the-dark paint, they didn't have to discuss which tunnel to go down, but just kept following the green arrows until they arrived in the whirlpool cave. Two bright lights were shining to the left of the whirlpool and, getting closer, they saw Kai and Coralie comforting Glenda, who was sitting on a boulder and crying. Her face was in her hands and her long hair was in a tangled mess round her shoulders. Bubbles was nudging anxiously at her tail, while Dash and Tommy were nosing curiously along the cave floor.

"Hey, guys! Over here!" Marina called, waving.

Kai and Coralie looked up, relief crossing their faces as they saw Marina and Naya.

"You're here and you're OK!" Coralie burst out.

"Yes, we're fine. How come you're all here?" demanded Marina.

"And what's the matter with Glenda?" said Naya.

"She banged her head quite badly on a rock when she flew out of the whirlpool," said Coralie.

Glenda looked up, dropping her hands and revealing a nasty cut above her eye.

Naya swam up to her. "You poor thing, Glenda. That looks really sore."

While Naya examined Glenda's wound, Marina asked Coralie again why the three of them had come through the whirlpool.

"Glenda saw you and Naya vanish and she wanted to get help. She was swimming to the meeting where all the adults were when Kai and I bumped into her. We'd finished our homework and were coming to look for you," said Coralie. "Anyway, when she told us what had happened, we grabbed some lanterns and decided to come and find you ourselves."

Kai chipped in. "We thought that if we

told the grown-ups you'd get into all sorts of trouble so we decided not to fetch them. Glenda insisted on coming too."

"I just wanted to help," sobbed Glenda. "I thought it would be an adventure, but I'm not sure I like adventures after all!"

"Where are we?" said Kai, glancing around curiously.

"We think we're in Mexico in an underground river." Marina explained about the network of caves while Naya put her arm round Glenda and hugged her. "The caves are just *spray-mazing*! Particularly one we found that is open-topped – it's got jungle all around it. I saw birds with really bright feathers and a furry creature that swung by its arms through the trees – Naya said it was a monkey!"

"Oh wow!" said Coralie. "That sounds *fin-credible*!"

Glenda gave a sob. "My head hurts!" Bubbles wriggled up into her arms and nuzzled her face sympathetically.

"I wish I had my first-aid kit with me," said Naya. "But I might have something in my bag that I can use as a bandage to stop the bleeding." She started to rummage in her bag and pulled out a wide roll of strong ribbon seaweed. "Yes, here we are. It would be better if I had some wound ointment too, but this will just have to do."

Octavia tugged her arm and then pointed back at the tunnel. When Naya frowned, not understanding, Octavia touched the freshly healed wound on Naya's hand, mimed picking something and then pointed backwards again, jiggling up and down excitedly.

"I get it!" said Naya suddenly. She looked at Marina. "Octavia thinks we should get some of the leaves that I was looking at when the graze on my hand healed. They might help with Glenda's wound."

"Let's go," said Marina. "We'll show you the way," she told the others. "Come on!"

Kai and Coralie swam over but, as Glenda tried to join them, her face paled. "The cave's spinning!" she gasped.

"Sit down," said Naya, grabbing her arm and guiding her back to the rock. "I don't think Glenda can swim yet," she said to the others.

Marina thought quickly. "OK, you all stay here and Sami and I'll go and fetch some leaves."

"Can't Kai and I come?" Coralie pleaded.

"It'll be faster if I go on my own," said Marina. "We need to get the leaves for Glenda as quickly as possible." She felt bad saying no, but the place was so amazing she knew that Kai and Coralie would want to stop and stare at everything, just like she and Naya had. "Perhaps we can all go exploring when Glenda's feeling better," she suggested.

"I just want to go home," sobbed Glenda. "What if the whirlpool disappears and we're trapped here forever!"

Naya nodded. "Glenda's right. We shouldn't stay too long. Hurry, Marina! The leaves were on the big green bush next to the plant with the green, heart-shaped fruit. They are slightly silvery, fairly long and thin. Take my light with you and my bag to put the leaves in – be quick and follow the arrows."

"I will. Promise!" Marina checked Sami was holding on tightly and then she set off. She was a strong, fast swimmer and now she knew where she was going she raced confidently through the water with strong flicks of her tail. She emerged out of the darkness into the open-topped cave, blinking in the sudden light. Catching sight of the bush Naya had described, she swam over and, leaving Sami in the water, pulled herself out on to the rocks. She started picking handfuls of the leaves and stuffing them into Naya's bag. As she broke them off the branches, they released a strong, fresh scent. Marina breathed it in; she'd never smelled anything like it before. She was just about to slip back into the cool water when a movement in the shadows at the far side of the pool made her pause.

An animal with a grey-brown coat stepped cautiously out from between two trees. Its legs were slender and its dark eyes were huge. Its ears flicked warily as it looked around and then bent its head to drink. Marina stayed as still as a statue, not wanting to startle it. She watched as the beautiful animal drank from the clear pool. Suddenly its head shot up, its ears swivelling, its nostrils flaring. There was a rustle in the bushes between it and Marina and the vines trembled as if something large and heavy was stalking past.

The slender animal instantly spun round and bounded away, disappearing into the shadows again. Sensing its obvious fear, Marina dived into the safety of the water and in three strokes was at the centre of the pool. She stared at the bushes where she had seen the ominous movement. She didn't see anything, but once again the vines trembled, this time as if something large was slinking away.

Sami came bobbing over to Marina. She picked him up and tucked him into her hair. "Let's go!" she said, her heart beating fast. Turning, she raced back to the others.

Chapter Six
Gone!

"That's looking better already," said Naya as she peeked under the bandage to check Glenda's wound.

She was sitting with Marina and Glenda on the ledge that jutted out just beneath the surface of the water. Naya had used the cave wall and a rock to grind the leaves Marina had collected into a thick green paste. She had gently smoothed some of it on to Glenda's forehead. It had clearly stung, but Glenda had hugged Bubbles tightly and not cried out. Naya had then bandaged Glenda's forehead.

Afterwards she and Marina sat with Glenda while Coralie and Kai investigated the cave, swimming round its rocky bottom, avoiding the whirlpool that swirled and frothed on the floor of the cave directly under the ledge. They had wanted to explore the tunnels, but had reluctantly decided it was better not to leave the cave, just in case the whirlpool looked like it was about to disappear.

The healing paste had worked quickly and colour was now starting to come back into Glenda's cheeks.

"How are you feeling?" Marina asked her.

"Better," said Glenda. "My head's much clearer now and not hurting nearly as much. Thanks for helping me." She looked around. "This is a really cool place." She pointed to the pot and the stone statue on the ledge beside them. "I think we're on a human offering shelf."

"What's an offering shelf?" said Marina.

Glenda stroked Bubbles gently. "Back in the olden days, humans put offerings to their gods in caves like this. The offerings were usually statues or jewellery, goblets or amulets. All sorts of precious objects. And often they were magical." She pointed upwards. "I think the humans must have used that rope ladder to climb down into the cave, and then left their gifts on the ledge."

"How do you know so much about humans?" asked Naya curiously.

"My mum used to study them," Glenda explained. "Before I was born, she was a researcher. She's told me about the places she's been and the things she's found out. It's one of the reasons I've always really wanted to travel – she made it sound so exciting. On her last trip, when she was swimming in the Amazon river near a human village, she got caught in a fishing net. She cut herself free just in time, but it was soon after I'd been born, and she decided she didn't want to have such a risky job any more so she gave it up. Daddy was pleased; he didn't like to think of her being in danger. It's why he never lets me travel either."

Marina and Naya exchanged looks. They'd never really chatted to Glenda before. It was strange to hear about her family. Marina felt like they were seeing a whole new side to her.

Glenda pulled a face. "Oh dear, I'm going to be in so much trouble when Daddy finds out I came through the whirlpool!"

"Maybe we can all get back without anyone realizing we've been gone," said Marina hopefully.

"We really should go now that you're feeling better, Glenda," said Naya.

Coralie and Kai came swimming up with Dash and Tommy. "Look what we just found!" said Coralie. She held up a beautiful green object. It was like a giant pendant from a necklace with four long slim cut outs. "It was on the bottom of the cave floor, near the edge of the whirlpool."

"I wonder what it is and what the humans did with it?" said Kai.

"I think it's an amulet," said Glenda. "Humans used them to channel magic in the olden days. It's exactly the sort of object they would have left as an offering to a god."

"Glenda was just telling us that humans used to have magical objects just like merpeople do," said Marina.

Glenda nodded. "Our magic and human magic isn't the same though. It's like the salt water and the fresh water: they're kind of the same but also different. Mer-magic and human magic don't mix."

"Why do you think this amulet was on the cave floor and not on the shelf with the other human things?" said Coralie.

Naya inspected the jagged edge of the shelf. "It looks like the ledge here has eroded. Maybe the amulet was at the end and it fell to the cave floor when the ledge crumbled."

"Let's put it back with the other objects," said Glenda.

Coralie placed the amulet beside the stone pot and looked longingly towards the tunnel marked with a green glowing arrow. "I wish we could go exploring. I'd love to see the place you told us about, with the butterflies and birds and monkeys."

Marina felt torn. She really wanted to go and explore some more too. "Maybe we could all stay just a little bit longer now Glenda's feeling better—" she started to say, but then she broke off as she noticed that the whirlpool beneath them had started to spin faster and faster. "Hey, look at that!"

"What's happening?" Glenda said uncertainly.

Dash whistled in alarm and Octavia swam into Naya's arms.

"I really think we should leave," said Naya nervously.

But, before any of them could move, the whirlpool dissolved into a stream of bubbles that popped and disappeared and then the water became still again. The whirlpool had completely vanished!

"It's gone!" gasped Coralie.

Marina's spirits plummeted like a stone as she stared at the space where the whirlpool had been. This was really not good at all. They were trapped in the cave with no way home!

"What are we going to do?" said Glenda. "Without it, we can't get back."

"Let's not panic," said Marina, swallowing. "It'll probably come back soon."

"*Probably?*" said Glenda, her voice rising.

"I'm almost definitely certain it will," said Marina, trying to sound confident to keep the others calm. "The mermaid who got caught down here said it vanished and then reappeared a little while later. We'll be fine."

She saw the fear on the others' faces and realized they needed a distraction. "How about we go exploring and then, when we come back, I bet you anything the whirlpool will be swirling away as normal and we'll be able to go home?"

"It would be lots of fun to explore," said Coralie slowly.

"Definitely," said Kai.

"It's a lot better than just waiting around here for the whirlpool to reappear," said Naya. She looked at Glenda. "What do think, Glenda? Are you going to come exploring?"

"You said you wanted an adventure," Marina reminded her.

"And I bet Bubbles would like it," added Naya.

Bubbles pushed his head hopefully against Glenda's arm. She hesitated for a moment and then lifted her chin. "All right," she said. "Let's go!"

Chapter Seven
Danger Lurks

"Oh, flippers! This place is *clam-tastic*!" breathed Glenda, swimming into the centre of the open pool and staring, wide-eyed, at the jungle. Bubbles stayed close to her side. The baby dolphin had been quite scared in the dark tunnels and Glenda had needed to encourage him along, stroking him and talking to him. Marina could tell that Glenda was getting quite fond of Bubbles.

"I've never been surrounded by land before!" said Coralie, gazing around.

"Look at those creepers – they'd be perfect for swinging from!" said Kai. "Come on, Coralie!" He swam over to the rocks where the vines were hanging down like thick ropes. He pulled himself out of the water on to the rocks and Coralie followed him.

"Be careful, you two!" exclaimed Glenda. "There might be humans about."

"It's OK. I think it's safe here," said Naya. "I had a good look around before and there are no signs that humans come here – no footprints or litter, no path leading to the pool."

Glenda nodded, reassured.

"It's so much fun here!" whooped Kai as he and Coralie took turns to grab a creeper and swing out over the pool before dropping in with a huge splash.

"I love this place!" cried Coralie.

Marina went to join them while Naya began to pick more leaves and put them in her bag, writing notes as she did so. Octavia, Dash and Tommy played chase in the crystal-clear water and Sami said hello to some giant river snails with dark green spiral shells.

Bubbles swam cautiously away from Glenda and stuck his nose in a bush covered with orange flowers at the side of the pool. He leaped backwards in surprise as two huge butterflies flew up into the air and fluttered away.

"Come and have a go at creeper-swinging, Glenda," said Marina, beckoning her over.

"I'm not sure it's for me," Glenda began uncertainly.

Marina laughed. "You'll never know unless you try it. Come on!"

She pulled Glenda through the water and helped her wriggle out on to a smooth slab of rock. Then she handed her a long, trailing vine. "Here you are – now off you go!" She gave her a hefty push.

Glenda squealed and clung on tightly to the creeper as she swung out across the water. She bobbed back and forth a few times before she let go and splashed into the pool. She emerged, shaking droplets of water from her eyes, her face alight. "Jumping jellyfish! That was so much fun!"

"Told you," grinned Marina, grabbing a vine herself and pushing off.

"Hey, everyone! I recognize this fruit from a book I read," said Naya as Marina splashed in. "It's called guanábana. You can eat it. Come and try it – it tastes delicious."

They all swam over and scrambled out next to an evergreen tree that had pale green fruit hanging from its branches. Around its base lay a pile of yellowing fruit that had ripened and fallen off. Naya had taken one from the branches and pulled it in half. The outside was tough and slightly spiky, but the inside was soft and white with some large black pips.

"It's really sweet and juicy!" Naya said, taking another bite. "Try some, everyone." She picked more fruit from the branches and handed them out.

Marina had never tasted anything like it before. Naya was right. It was absolutely scrumptious! She ate one fruit and then picked another up from the pile on the ground. This one was much softer and squishier and, as she bit into it, she pulled a face. "Yuck! This one's rotten!" she spluttered, spitting out the mouthful she had just taken.

"Here, try this one instead," said Naya, picking a fresh one from the branches.

They ate until they couldn't eat a mouthful

more and then washed their hands and faces in the water.

"Where's Bubbles?" said Glenda, looking around.

"Over there," said Marina, spotting the baby dolphin nosing his way down a narrow channel of water that cut through the rocks on the far side of the pool. "Silly thing! He's going to get stuck if he goes down there. It's much too narrow."

As she spoke, Bubbles stopped – his plump, round body was wedged in between the rocks on either side and he couldn't go either forwards or back. He bucked up and down, trying to free himself, but was firmly jammed in.

"I'll go and rescue him," said Glenda, smiling. But, just as she started to swim across the pool to the baby dolphin, Marina saw the branches on the bushes next to the channel quiver. Something large was pushing its way stealthily through them towards Bubbles.

An image of the startled animal bounding away earlier flashed into her mind and suddenly she was sure that whatever was in the bushes was very dangerous. "Glenda! Be careful!" she shouted, feeling a sharp stab of fear.

Glenda looked round in surprise. "Why? What's—" She broke off with a horrified gasp as a giant cat with dark circles on its golden coat sprang out of the bushes and bounded across the rocks towards Bubbles.

Marina froze. The animal was absolutely beautiful, but she could see at a glance that it was deadly. Its muscles rippled under its sleek fur, it had long claws and sharp teeth and its amber eyes were fixed hungrily on the little dolphin.

"It's a jaguar!" cried Naya.

"No!" Glenda screamed at the top of her voice as Bubbles started to thrash around in fear.

Her scream was so loud that the jaguar skidded to a surprised halt.

"Go away!" Glenda shrieked, swimming towards it, shaking her fists. "You leave Bubbles alone!" She pulled off her bag and threw it at the jaguar. It landed at its feet and the creature recoiled in surprise.

Marina grabbed one of the rotten fruits and hurled it at as hard as she could at the big cat. It splattered on the ground by its large paws. The jaguar started to back away.

Everyone else joined in, grabbing handfuls of fruit and pelting the jaguar with them.

"Go on!"

"Get away!"

"Leave Bubbles alone!"

Glenda swam closer, screaming so loudly that the leaves on the nearby trees shook. The jaguar decided it had had enough. Flattening its ears against its head, it turned and bounded away into the jungle.

"Oh, Bubbles!" gasped Glenda, reaching the frightened baby dolphin and gently easing him out of the narrow channel. "I thought you were going to be eaten!" She wrapped her arms round the little animal and hugged him.

Bubbles tried to hide underneath Glenda's long hair, messing it up, but Glenda didn't care. She swam back to the others, the dolphin in her arms.

"Wow! You were brilliant, Glenda!" said Kai.

"You saved Bubbles," said Marina, swimming to meet her.

"Without you, it really could have been a *big cat*-astrophe!" Coralie said.

Glenda smiled as the pets nuzzled and nosed at Bubbles, checking he was OK.

"You were so brave, Glenda," said Naya.

Kai nodded. "The way you swam straight at that jaguar was awesome."

Glenda flushed, looking almost embarrassed at the praise. "I thought the jaguar was going to eat Bubbles and I couldn't bear it." A grin crossed her face. "It didn't like my screaming much, did it?"

"It really didn't," said Marina with a grin. "Poor jaguar."

Naya swam over and retrieved Glenda's bag from the rocks. "I can't believe you even threw your precious mirror and comb at it," she said, handing the bag back. "Here, look, they're still safe inside."

"Bubbles is much more precious than any mirror or comb," said Glenda, kissing the top of Bubbles' head. Bubbles snuggled closer and Glenda smiled.

"We should probably get back before we meet anything else dangerous," said Naya.

Kai nodded. "I wonder if the whirlpool's come back yet."

"Let's go and check," said Coralie.

As Kai, Coralie and Glenda swam into the tunnel that led back to the whirlpool cave, Naya pulled on Marina's arm and they dropped back slightly. "Marina, what are we going to do if the whirlpool doesn't ever reappear?" she whispered anxiously.

Marina's stomach twisted into a tight knot.

She'd been trying not to think about that because she really didn't know the answer. Without the whirlpool, there was no way back to Mermaids Rock. They would be trapped in the caves forever!

Chapter Eight

Whirlpools and Magic

As they swam into the whirlpool cave, they all stopped. The water at the bottom of the cave was still and there was no sign of the whirlpool. Marina's heart sank. She could see from the expression on her friends' faces that they were just as alarmed.

"It… It's still not here," said Coralie, her voice shaky for once.

"What are we going to do?" said Kai, swimming over to the place where the whirlpool had been.

Dash, Tommy and Bubbles nudged at the cave floor as if they were hoping they could make the whirlpool reappear. Octavia scratched her head with two of her arms and Sami zoomed round the cave, searching for another whirlpool hidden somewhere.

Glenda swallowed hard. "If it doesn't appear, will we have to stay here forever?"

"I'm sure that won't happen," said Marina quickly. "It's bound to come back very soon."

She looked hopefully at Naya. "I don't suppose you happen to know of any scientific way of getting whirlpools back if they vanish, Naya?"

"No," said Naya, shaking her head slowly. "I've never heard of whirlpools disappearing before. I've no idea what we can do."

"Well, maybe someone back home will solve the mystery," said Marina optimistically. "Yes, that's it. They'll get the whirlpool working again, it'll suddenly appear and we'll all be able to travel back home to the reef, no problem."

The others nodded slowly. It was the only hope they had.

"I've got some emergency sea humbugs in my bag," said Naya. "Why don't we sit on the ledge and share those?"

They all swam slowly up to the jutting-out ledge where the human objects and handprints were. Bubbles went with them. He seemed to like staying close to Glenda. While Naya got the sea humbugs out of her bag, Coralie picked up the amulet she and Kai had found on the cave floor. "Humans do have really different things," she said. "I wonder what this magic thing can do?"

"Amulets were usually used for magical protection or to get from one place to another," said Glenda. "Can I have another look at it?" She reached out to take it from Coralie but, as she did so, Bubbles nudged her arm, looking for cuddles, and the amulet fell from her fingers and started to sink towards the cave floor.

"Oh, Bubbles, you clumsy thing!" exclaimed Glenda, pretending to be annoyed, but stroking the little dolphin and kissing his nose.

"Tommy can get it. Tommy, fetch!" said Kai. Tommy looked up from where he was nosing at the rocky floor and glanced enquiringly at Kai. "The amulet, Tommy. Bring it here to me."

Tommy spotted the golden amulet as it fell and swooped to pick it up in his mouth just as it hit the cave floor. As he grabbed it, a golden spark flew off its sides and the water nearby started to ripple and slowly spin.

"The whirlpool!" Marina gasped loudly. "It's coming back. Look!"

But as Tommy swam up towards them the water became still again. Everyone, apart from Naya, groaned in dismay.

"It's gone again,' said Coralie.

"Why did it come and go like that?" said Glenda.

"I've absolutely no idea," said Marina in frustration.

Naya stared at the floor of the cave, frowning. Then she looked at Tommy, who was putting the golden amulet into Kai's hands. "Hang on!" she said suddenly. "Kai, can I have that for a moment?"

Kai handed it over. "Sure."

Holding the amulet, Naya dived from the ledge and swam down to the floor. She touched the amulet to the rocks there. The amulet seemed to sparkle for a moment and then the waters started to swirl. Naya swam backwards with the amulet, keeping it touching the floor. The whirlpool built up speed. "It's the amulet!" Naya cried. "It's affecting the whirlpool."

"It's made the whirlpool come back!" whooped Marina. She turned to the others, her eyes shining. "We can get home after all."

They dived down and joined Naya at the edge of the whirlpool.

"The amulet's magic must react with the whirlpool's magic in some way," Naya said, watching the swirling, frothing water. "I don't understand it, but there's definitely a link."

"Who cares why it's happening? The important thing is that we can get home," said Kai, high-fiving Coralie.

"Let's all dive in at the same time, just in case it takes us somewhere other than Mermaids Rock," said Marina. "We don't want to be split up. Are you all ready?" Her friends nodded. "Then one... Two..."

"Wait!" exclaimed Naya. "There's something deep down in the whirlpool – something glittering and shining. Look!"

Marina looked. The depths of the magic whirlpool went far deeper than the rocky floor. As she peered into the swirling waters, she saw what Naya was pointing at. Something golden was glittering far below. "It looks like another amulet," she said, surprised. “What’s it doing there?”

Naya’s eyes lit up. “I think we might just have solved the mystery of the malfunctioning whirlpool! I bet the amulet that’s inside the whirlpool was once on the ledge above us, but when the ledge crumbled it fell into the water, affecting the way the whirlpool’s magic works.” She turned to Glenda. “You said human and mer-magic don’t mix?”

Glenda nodded.

Naya smiled triumphantly. “Well, that’s probably why the whirlpool isn’t working then. The amulet is interfering with the flow of magic.”

Marina frowned. “So what can we do?”

“Get it out,” said Naya as if it was obvious.

Marina stared into the depths of the bubbling whirlpool. “But how do we do that?”

Chapter Nine

A Dangerous Mission

They all gazed at the glittering amulet in the depths of the whirlpool. "Do we really have to get it out?" said Glenda slowly. "Why don't we just use the whirlpool to go home and then get the guards to deal with it?"

"For a start, if the whirlpool magic isn't working properly, we might not get home – we might end up somewhere else in the world entirely," said Marina. "But the main reason why we have to do it is because the only way to get the amulet out is from this cave here, isn't it, Naya?"

Naya nodded. "If your father and the guards had been able to see the amulet from the main whirlpool at Mermaids Rock, I'm sure they would have realized it was causing the problem and pulled it out already, Glenda."

"Which means we're the only ones who can get to it," said Marina, her eyes flashing with determination. "We've saved the day before," she said, looking at Coralie, Kai and Naya. "It's time to do it again!"

"The trouble is," Coralie pointed out, "it's really far down. If one of us dives in, we might be whisked away somewhere else before we can grab it."

Marina remembered how fast the whirlpool had spun her when it had brought her here. One moment she'd been at Mermaids Rock and the next she'd been shooting out into the cave. Coralie was right: if they dived into this whirlpool, there was a danger they would simply be transported somewhere else before they could do anything about it.

"We need a way of diving in without being instantly taken somewhere else," she said, thinking aloud.

"A mer-chain!" cried Glenda. They looked at her. "We form a chain – someone dives in, someone else holds on to their tail, someone else holds on to them, and so on," she explained. "We make a long line, with the last person staying here in the cave. If everyone hangs on tight, then the first person can grab the amulet and be pulled back safely."

"Or we all get sucked in and end up scattered around the world," said Coralie doubtfully.

"It is very risky," said Marina, scratching her head. "The current in the whirlpool is so strong that we might not be able to hold on to each other."

"We need something we could tie ourselves together with to make it safer," said Naya.

"If only there was some seaweed."

Marina looked round the empty cave. "But there's no seaweed anywhere here."

"There isn't," said Kai. "But what about those vines? The ones we were swinging on by the pool were super-strong. Couldn't we use them instead of seaweed?"

Marina high-fived him. "That's a brilliant idea, Kai!"

"Let's go and get some right now," said Glenda eagerly.

"It might be best if just Coralie and Marina go," said Naya. "They're the fastest swimmers. If we all go, it'll take longer."

Everyone agreed and so Marina and Coralie raced back to the open pool. Keeping their eyes peeled for the scary jaguar, they cut down some creepers, using a sharp rock as a knife, and then carried armfuls back to the cave.

Sitting in a circle, they all plaited the vines together to form a strong rope.

"OK, who's going to dive in first?" said Coralie when they were all securely attached to each other with the creepers knotted round their waists.

"I will," said Marina. "Who'll go behind me and hang on to my tail?"

"Me," said Coralie.

They decided on the order of Marina, Coralie, Kai and Glenda, with Naya staying outside the whirlpool and anchoring them all. Naya tied the end of the rope that dangled from her waist round a hefty rock near the whirlpool that was sticking up from the floor like a pillar and then it was time for Marina to dive in.

"It might be safer if you stayed here in the cave with Naya until I'm back," Marina told Sami.

But the little seahorse shook his head stubbornly and swam into her hair. She felt him wrap his tail firmly round the lock behind her ear. "OK, OK. I guess where I go, you come too," she said. She felt his little head nod firmly against her neck.

"It's funny, I never really understood why you lot had pets," said Glenda, stroking Bubbles who was beside her. "They just seemed a lot of hassle – taking care of them, training them, making sure they're safe and all that stuff – but now I think I get it."

Naya smiled. "We look after them and they look after us," she said, stroking Octavia, who was hugging her.

"They make us laugh," said Kai.

"And we have all sorts of fun with them," added Coralie.

Dash and Tommy clapped their flippers in agreement.

"They're also our best friends," said Marina softly, tickling Sami's tail.

She felt him nod.

Glenda looked thoughtfully at Bubbles.

"Right, let's get this amulet," said Naya. "Then all of us – and our pets – can get back safe and sound to the reef."

Marina looked at the rushing, bubbling water. "Are we ready?" she asked.

"Ready!" her friends chorused.

You can do this, Marina told herself. *You have to!*

Bracing herself, she dived in, with Coralie hanging on to her tail, and then Kai and Glenda followed. As Marina's arms entered the whirlpool, she felt the rushing water trying

to whip her away. *No*, she thought, fighting against the current. *You're not taking me somewhere else.* Forcing her eyes to stay open, she focused on the glittering amulet far beneath her. The whirlpool pummelled and buffeted her, the water roaring in her ears, but she swam strongly downwards with swift strokes. Her hands reached out. For a moment, she thought the whirlpool was going to snatch her away, but then her fingers closed on metal.

She'd got it!

She flicked her tail fin – a signal they'd agreed in advance. Hanging on tightly to the amulet, she felt Coralie start to haul her backwards. However, the whirlpool began to spin even faster and Marina felt Coralie's hands slip from her tail. For a heart-stopping moment, she thought she was going to be transported somewhere else, but then felt a sharp jerk at her waist as the creeper rope tightened and held her fast. Coralie's hands grasped her tail again and, little by little, her friends pulled her out of the rushing water.

As Marina was hauled back into the cave with the amulet in her hands, the whirlpool started to slow down to normal speed. She breathed a huge sigh of relief.

"We did it!" she cried, holding the amulet up.

Everyone cheered and the animals bounced around in delight. Tommy, Dash and Bubbles turned happy somersaults while Octavia waved her arms and Sami, having let go of Marina's hair, zoomed around like a miniature golden arrow.

"I think we should put both the amulets well away from the whirlpool," said Naya, taking Marina's and picking the other one off the floor.

She swam up to the offering shelf and placed them next to the goblet and statue, as close to the cave wall as possible. To make absolutely sure they stayed there and didn't fall off again, she fetched some small rocks to make a barrier round them. Octavia helped by fetching more stones and pushing them firmly into place.

"Hopefully, they'll be safe there now," said Naya, swimming back to the others. "No more falling into the whirlpool and making it go wrong. You were right, Glenda: human and mer-magic really don't mix."

"We solved the mystery,' said Marina,

delight fizzing through her.

"And we've had a *fin-tabulous* adventure!" said Coralie.

"I really think this has been the best day of my entire life!" said Glenda, her eyes shining.

"It won't be when we get home," said Kai. "The grown-ups are bound to have realized we've vanished."

"We're going to be in so much trouble," groaned Coralie.

They all exchanged worried looks.

"Well, we can't stay here forever so we'd better go and face them," said Marina bravely. "Come on, everyone!" She swam to the edge of the whirlpool and waited for them all to join her, then she counted them down. "One… Two… Three… GO!"

Together, they dived into the gently swirling water.

Marina was very relieved to find that travelling through the whirlpool felt just as it usually did. The waters swirled her around, but this time they were gentle with her. The bubbles seemed to stroke her hair and skin rather than clawing and grabbing at her, and a cloud of beautiful rainbow light encircled her. She tumbled out into warm turquoise water and saw the familiar sight of Mermaids Rock rearing up from the ocean floor. Shoals of purple and yellow fish swooped by her nose and a manta ray glided underneath her. Relief flooded through her. She was home!

With shouts and cries, Coralie, Glenda, Kai and Naya all came spinning out of the whirlpool along with the animals.

"We got back," said Coralie in delight, flicking her tail and turning herself the right way up. Dash clapped his flippers, whistling happily, and little Bubbles copied.

"We're all safe!" exclaimed Naya as Octavia swam out of her arms.

"We are and guess what?" said Marina, glancing around. "There are no grown-ups here!" she exclaimed, delighted. She'd been expecting to arrive back and have to face a ring of angry guards and a furious Chief Razeem.

"Do you think we might have got away with it?' said Kai.

"Oh, I hope so," said Glenda.

"We should get away from here fast," urged

Marina. "I guess they've all been too busy to notice we'd gone."

But, as they started to swim quickly away from the whirlpool, there was a loud shout. "There they are!"

Marine froze and looked round. A group of parents were swimming angrily towards them!

Chapter Ten

Facing the Music

The gang's parents whizzed out from all over the reef. Luna and Erin were with them and Luna reached Marina first, throwing her arms round her waist. "You're OK! Oh, I'm so glad!"

"Where have you all been?" cried Indra, Kai's mum. Her trident shook in her hand as she swam over and her forehead was creased with worry lines.

"We've been so worried. We had no idea where you were," said Erin. "We've been searching everywhere."

"Did you go in the whirlpool?" demanded Naya's dad.

"Um, yes," Naya admitted.

"Clattering clams! Whatever for?" exclaimed Coralie's dad.

"You know Chief Razeem said no one was to go near it!" said her mum.

Tarak, Marina's dad, pulled Marina close and kissed her hair. "I'm just glad you're safe, sweetheart," he said, hugging her. "You really had me worried there."

Marina hugged him back. "I am safe – we all are – and guess what, Dad? We solved—"

"GLENDA!" a voice roared. Chief Razeem came charging across the reef, his tail swishing furiously, his eyes glaring at her. He was followed by Glenda's mum, a beautiful blonde mermaid called Sasha.

"Glenda, darling! You're safe!" she cried. She overtook Razeem, accidentally knocking Bubbles as she hugged Glenda tightly.

"Mummy, mind Bubbles," Glenda gasped. She struggled free and went to check on the little dolphin. Bubbles quickly tucked himself under Glenda's arm. "He's from the sanctuary. I've been looking after him and he –" Glenda kissed Bubbles' head – "has been looking after me."

Bubbles wriggled in delight.

"Young lady, you are in big trouble," said Chief Razeem, shaking his trident at her. "Did you seriously go into the whirlpool?"

"Yes, Daddy, but—"

"YES?" Razeem exploded. "But Glenda, you knew it was out of bounds!" His dark eyes narrowed. "Did those other children force you to go with them? Is that it? Did they make you go?"

"No, Daddy. I went because I wanted to help," said Glenda. "It's not their fault so you mustn't blame them. Marina's seahorse got sucked in so she went after him and Naya followed. Coralie, Kai and I went to try to rescue them. Only we got trapped. The whirlpool at the other end disappeared and we couldn't come home."

"Which is exactly why everyone has been banned from using the whirlpool!" her father exclaimed. "Everyone knows that it is dangerous—"

"It's not dangerous any more, Chief Razeem," Marina interrupted him. "We've solved the mystery!"

"You've done what?" The chief glared at her down his long nose, but she stared right back. She wasn't frightened of him.

"We didn't just solve the mystery, we fixed the problem too," declared Glenda. "So please stop shouting, Daddy, and just listen to us."

Chief Razeem blinked, looking thoroughly taken aback.

Glenda's mum tucked her arm through his. "Maybe we should hear what Glenda and the others have to say?"

"Very well." Chief Razeem cleared his throat and then spoke gruffly. "Go on.

You may explain."

Glenda, along with Marina and occasional additions from Coralie, Kai and Naya, told the adults everything that had happened. When they mentioned finding the amulet in the whirlpool, Sasha caught her breath.

"That makes perfect sense. Amulets channel magic. An amulet in the whirlpool would make the whole network of whirlpools malfunction because the magic would be pulled to that one point." She looked at Razeem. "That must be why everyone from Mermaids Rock kept ending up in that cave. The other amulet that had fallen on the floor would have made things worse. The two amulets would have been trying to connect and that would have sent the whirlpool haywire."

"So you removed the amulet from the whirlpool?" Tarak said quickly to Marina.

"Yes, we left it in the cave on the offering

shelf, where it should have been all along."

Tarak nodded. "Very wise. It would have been very dangerous to have tried to come through the whirlpool with it, and it's always best to leave things as undisturbed as possible when you travel through the world." He looked at Chief Razeem. "It appears the children have done us all a great favour, Razeem. They have solved the mystery *and* fixed the problem."

"The whirlpool is now working just perfectly again," said Marina happily.

Chief Razeem looked as if he didn't know quite what to say. "I … er … um…"

"Well done, all of you!" Sasha interrupted, beaming at them. "You've been incredibly brave and resourceful by the sound of it and we should be thanking you, shouldn't we, Razeem?"

"Well. Yes, I suppose." Razeem swallowed as though he had something sharp in his throat. "Well done, children," he said stiffly.

"Thank you."

Their parents hugged them and Glenda kissed her dad's cheek. "See, it all worked out perfectly and there was absolutely no need to be cross, Daddy."

"I think a celebration is called for!" said her mum. "We've still got almost a whole birthday cake left over from Glenda's birthday yesterday. Won't you all come to our cave and have a piece?"

"*Clam-tastic!* I could bring along the sea-lemon tart I made today," said Naya's dad.

"And I have some seaweed biscuits," said Coralie's mum. "I can pick them up on the way."

Glenda's mum beamed. "Wonderful! We can have a proper celebration tea."

"I'll drop Bubbles back at the sanctuary first," said Erin. "Come along, Bubbles."

Bubbles shook his head and nestled closer to Glenda.

“Come along, you silly thing,” said Erin, smiling.

Bubbles hid behind Glenda and ducked under her curtain of long hair.

Erin began to swim over. “Bubbles, you really do have to come with me.”

“Wait,” Glenda said quickly. “Mum? Dad?” She looked at her parents. “You know you got me a mirror and comb for my birthday?”

“Yes,” her dad said, looking bemused.

“Well, there’s a present I’d really, really like instead. You can have the mirror and comb back. This is the only thing I really want.”

"What is?" asked her mum.

Marina exchanged looks with Naya and the others. She had a feeling she knew what Glenda was about to say.

"Bubbles," said Glenda softly, lifting her hair out of the way and stroking the dolphin. "I want him to be my pet."

Bubbles peeped round Glenda and looked at Sasha and Razeem appealingly.

Marina saw them glance at each other as if not sure what to do. "Having a pet is an excellent way of learning about responsibility," she said quickly.

"Yes," Naya added. "You learn so much from looking after an animal."

"And our pets help keep us safe," said Coralie.

Kai and Luna nodded.

Sasha looked at Razeem. "You know I've been thinking for a while that it would be good for Glenda to have a pet. I used to have a dolphin when I was growing up and I had so much fun with him. I think we should let her keep Bubbles." She glanced at Erin. "If that's OK with you of course, Erin?"

Erin smiled. "It's absolutely fine. Bubbles needs a home and it's clear how much he has taken to Glenda."

"Please, Daddy," Glenda begged. "Say yes!"

Chief Razeem's usual stern expression softened into something that looked almost like a smile. "Very well," he said. "Yes!"

The Save the Sea Creatures Club high-fived each other as Glenda squealed in delight and hugged Bubbles. "Oh, Bubbles, you're the best birthday present ever! I'm going to look after you and love you! I'll be the best owner ever!"

Bubbles whistled in delight. Breaking free of Glenda, he whizzed away across the reef.

"Bubbles! Come back!" called Glenda, racing after him.

Marina giggled. "I think Glenda's going to be kept busy with the looking-after part," she said.

"*Dolphin-itely*!" said Coralie with a grin.

Naya groaned.

"Time for tea, everyone!" said Sasha.

"Maybe we could play *salmon says* or *murder in the shark*!" said Coralie.

"It's definitely time to go if Coralie's telling jokes," said Coralie's dad, shaking his head.

Everyone set off towards the Seaglasses' cave, talking and laughing.

"I can't believe you had an adventure without me," said Luna, swimming with the rest of the gang. "It's so unfair! I want to hear about all the animals you saw. You need to tell me everything!"

"We will and we'll take you there one day," promised Naya.

"So long as you promise not to try and cuddle a jaguar!" said Marina.

"Yes, even you might think their teeth looked pretty *roar-ful*, Luna!" said Coralie, grinning.

Kai splashed her with his tail fin. "It's your jokes that are *roar-ful*, Coralie!"

"Ha ha!" she said, flicking him back. "With friends like you, who needs *an-enemies*! Race you all to Glenda's cave!"

Leaving the whirlpool swirling peacefully behind them, the five of them sped away with their pets beside them. Weaving swiftly through the warm, bright coral world, Marina felt a rush of pure happiness. They'd had an amazing adventure and now they were all home, safe and sound.

I'm so lucky, she thought as she dodged round a pair of slow-moving manatees and took a short cut through a gap in the coral. *I live in the best place in the world and I have the best friends in the world and I bet there's another* fin-tastic *adventure just waiting round the corner!*

She flicked her tail in delight. She couldn't wait to find out what it would be!

Turn the page to learn more about cenotes and the creatures that live there!

CENOTES

A cenote is a natural sinkhole. They are mainly found on the Yucatán Peninsula in Mexico where there are an estimated 6,000! Cenotes are formed when the porous limestone bedrock collapses, revealing the secret pool below. They can be connected by underground cave systems.

Cave cenotes usually have fresh water, filtered by the earth. They are so clear you can see the fish and plant life right at the bottom! Cave systems as well as stalactites and stalagmites make them exciting to explore. Open-air cenotes have clear water as well, but they also contain vitamin and mineral-rich algae.

The Maya (indigenous people of Mexico and Central America) valued and respected cenotes. Cenotes were the only source of water in the jungle, so settlements grew round the sinkholes.

The Maya considered cenotes sacred, believing them to be a portal through which they could speak with the gods. Archaeologists have discovered ritual offering chambers in the underground cave systems where there the Maya left artefacts, including incense burners, decorative plates and vases.

Nowadays, people visit cenotes to swim, dive and explore. These beautiful turquoise pools offer a chance to experience nature in a unique way – swimming under the jungle, with bats circling above and fish nibbling swimmers' feet below.

BATS

Marina gets a shock when she's exploring the caves and meets a colony of bats!

Bats are the only mammals that can fly – and they're really good at it! Bats have four long fingers and a thumb, which are covered in a thin membrane. They fly by spreading out their long digits and flapping!

To make their way around the dark caves, bats use echolation. The bats make high-pitched sounds that travels until they hit something. When it bounces back to them, they can judge how big and far away the object is based on the echo.

Bats are nocturnal. They spend their days resting in roosts. Roosts can be found in cracks and crevices where they're protected. When the bats roost, they hang upside down from their hind feet and legs.

Bats are really important for humans and the environment. Bats that eat insects can consume millions of bugs a night, which acts as natural pest control for plants. Nectar-drinking bats pollinate plants, which helps to produce fruit. There are actually more than 500 species of plant that rely on bats for pollination! And fruit-eating bats can also help to spread seeds. This helps rainforests grow and can counter effects of deforestation. So despite bats having a reputation for being spooky, they're amazing and important creatures.

Collect them all and dive into Mermaids Rock!

Linda Chapman
Mirelle Ortega
Mermaids
Rock
The Coral Kingdom

Linda Chapman
Mirelle Ortega
Mermaids
Rock
The Floating Forest

Linda Chapman
Mirelle Ortega
Mermaids
Rock
The Ice Giant

Linda Chapman
Mirelle Ortega
Mermaids
Rock
The Midnight Realm

About the Author

Linda Chapman is the best-selling author of over 200 books. The biggest compliment Linda can receive is for a child to tell her they became a reader after reading one of her books. Linda lives in a cottage with a tower in Leicestershire with her husband, three children, three dogs and two ponies. When she's not writing, Linda likes to ride, read and visit schools and libraries to talk to people about writing.

www.lindachapmanauthor.co.uk

About the Illustrator

Mirelle Ortega is a Mexican artist based in Los Angeles. She has a MFA in Visual Development from the Academy of Art University in San Francisco. Mirelle loves magic, vibrant colours and ghost stories. But more than anything, she loves telling unique stories with funny characters and a touch of magical realism.

www.mirelleortega.com

JOIN MARINA AND HER FRIENDS FOR THEIR NEXT ADVENTURE IN...

COMING SOON!